the day after Yesterday

story + pictures
by
Phyllis Rowand

34464

the day after Yesterday

THERE IS a little girl.

She lives in the country, in a house that looks a little like a party cake, a little house touching the water.

In the water live ducks, minnows, flounder, bluefish, blackfish, blowfish, and sometimes jellyfish.

There are hermit crabs, fiddler crabs, lobster, horseshoe crabs and plain crabby crabs, the kind that pinch when they are frightened.

There are also all the endless other lives that live in and under water.

Snails, clams, quahogs, oysters.

Sand hoppers, shellfish, limpets, periwinkles.

Mussels, barnacles, starfish.

And other sea things so small they almost cannot be seen.

And sea gulls live over the water.

And over them drift lazy cloud-birds.

Or quick bright white puffs that blow and tumble into easy animal shapes.

Or roll upon long roll of fleecy masses, called in books "cirro-cumulus," but which people say is a mackerel sky.

Inside the house, with the little girl and her mother and father, live a dog and a cat.

She used to have a rabbit, which also lived in the house, but it began to eat clothing and the kitchen linoleum, so her mother made her give it to a farmer, with whom it is said to be very happy.

In the bit of land around the house, in the places where it does not touch the water, there are, of course, worms and beetles and bugs among the flowers and vegetables.

Hoptoads, ants, anthills, crickets, katydids.

And over the bit of land are ladybugs, bumble-
bees and butterflies, sparrows and grackles, and
more bugs—those that have wings.

In the ailanthus tree a squirrel family lives, and mice scurry through the whispering sea grass.

The ailanthus is also called the Tree of Heaven.

These are the little girl's friends.

The snails, the fish, the squirrels, the ducks, the bugs, the birds, the mice, the minnows, all.

She talks to them and plays with them and gives them food.

She spends long hours catching minnows in milk bottles, using bread for bait.

At night she returns them to their own waters, for she has learned that they cannot live for long in a bucket.

When the tide goes out there is a half-moon of beach on one side of the house.

There the little girl molds villages of pebbles and sand for the crabs and starfish, the clams and snails—for whatever small creatures happen to be by the water's edge.

WIPE YOUR FEET
x
MOTHER

Rowayton News

STOP
MANRESA
SMOKE
MENACE

One day the mother stands in the doorway of the little house, watching the child outside.

The little girl has set sunflower seeds in circles on the grass.

The ducks, squirrels, birds, are all around her, pecking the sweet meat out of the shells, scolding each other, cackling and clucking as they follow the white dots in the green grass.

"You know what?" asks the mother, turning to the father.

"No, what?" answers the father.

"I think it is time for our child to learn that there is a world other than this one in her own back yard — a world full of people and many fine things created by people."

And so, sighing, they talk it over.

They decide that it would be good for her to see that there are many other sights just as wonderful as the hive of the honeybee, as beautiful as a nest of newborn birds, as exciting as the treasures left on the beach by the outgoing tide.

They sigh because they really do not want her to go, because they will miss her so.

But they decide to send her to visit her cousins in the city.

The mother makes her a pretty new dress, pink.

And a petticoat to go under it, all stiff with starch and ruffles and lace.

The dress has three velvet cherries on the bodice, and on her hat the mother sews three cherries too.

The mother braids her hair, and the father shines her shoes and they take the suitcase down out of the attic and they buy her a pocketbook, her very first.

It is the kind that has an over-the-shoulder strap.

She takes a train to the city, to the biggest city in the world.

There she is met by her cousins, who are very happy that she has come to visit.

They take her to see the many wonderful things that people go to the city to see . . .

She sees the tallest building in all the world, and goes swiftly up—up—up—to the very top of it . . .

And she goes down, down, down, to a train roaring under the ground.

She goes by boat to an island where there is a great bronze statue.

It is a woman offering welcome to all the lonely people who come here new from other lands.

She walks down a wide avenue of fine shops full of costly toys and other shining wares.

She sits awhile in a very large church.

She rides in a double-decker bus to a place like a palace. It is a museum.

Inside, there are jewels of real gold and articles of solid silver, marble statuettes and ornate ivory carvings.

There are stories woven into cloth, told long long ago, cherished for five hundred years.

On the last day of her visit she goes shopping for presents to bring home to her mother and father.

She shops carefully, looking and looking until she finds just what she wants to take home from the biggest city in the world.

And she carries the gifts carefully on her lap on the train all the long journey home.

When she arrives at the little house that touches the water she kisses her mother and her father and gives them the presents she has brought.

Then she runs out to the yellow velvet sun, to the bright water, to the garden warm with many colors.

She stands and listens to the happy hubbub of greeting—the sweet sounds of her friends welcoming her home—the barking, the scolding, the cackling, the buzzing, the peeping, the chattering, the shrilling, the purring.

She hears too the quiet of those who cannot speak.

She hears them because she knows that they are there.

And in and around and over and under and through those sounds there is at all times the steady roll of the waves touching the house, the wall, the beach.

There is the low whisper of the tall sea grass.

There are little bright white clouds, tumbling high.

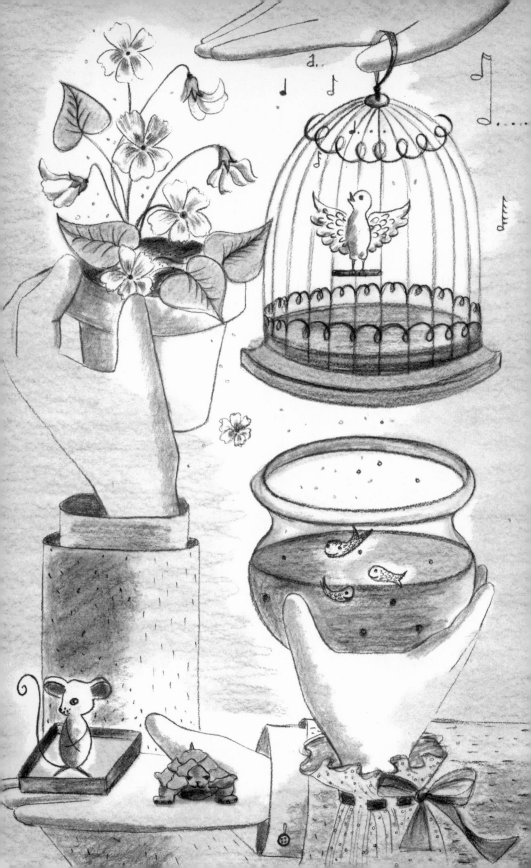

Now the mother and father are coming out of the house and into the garden too.

They have unwrapped their presents and are holding them in their hands.

They are very happy to have the gifts she has chosen to bring them out of all the many many things there are to choose from in the biggest city in the world.

In their hands they hold—

>a plant of purple violets
>a green turtle
>a small white mouse
>a yellow singing bird
>and
>three goldfish.

The little girl sees the happiness in their faces as they bend down to kiss her again, and then again.

But if she had *not* seen their happiness she might be thinking that they have tears in their eyes—

Because their eyes are *that* shining bright . . .